c.1   ++

Davis

Any cat can cook   gr.2

GARFIELD

GARFIELD

LEARNS ABOUT COOKING
Any Cat Can Cook

Created by Jim Davis
Story by Mark Acey
Illustrated by Paws, Inc.

A GOLDEN BOOK • NEW YORK
Western Publishing Company, Inc.
Racine, Wisconsin 53404

"I'm going now," said Jon to Garfield and Odie. "I won't be back until this evening, so I've left some food in your dishes. Don't wreck the house while I'm gone."

"Don't worry," said Garfield. "We'll leave the walls standing."

Garfield and Odie dashed into the kitchen to see what Jon had left for them.

"Cat food?" grumbled Garfield. "Get real!"

Meanwhile, Odie was already shoveling in his food.

"Anything's good enough for a dog," thought Garfield. "But *my* stomach deserves something better. Something as special and wonderful as I am. Hmmm, let me see. I know, lasagna! Or cookies! Or better yet—LASAGNA COOKIES!"

Odie came bounding across the room with a cookbook. "Thanks, Odie," said Garfield. "But I don't need a recipe. I am a master chef! Yessir, Garfield's my name and cooking's my game. Besides, recipes are too complicated and take much too long. And I'm starving!"

Garfield went to the cupboard and took out his favorite ingredients. Then he went to the refrigerator and took out his other favorite ingredients. Then he took all of his favorite ingredients and dumped them into a big bowl.

"Now we're cookin'," said Garfield as Odie looked on in amazement. "Bring me the mixer. I'm going to whip this stuff into shape."

Garfield began to beat the batter—and then eat the batter.

"Not bad," he thought. "A little on the heavy side, but then so am I."

"Arf," barked Odie, offering Garfield a cookie cutter.

"No time for fancy stuff," said Garfield.

Garfield then poured the batter into a baking dish—and all over the floor.

"Oops," said Garfield, "too much batter, not enough dish. Guess I should have measured the ingredients after all. Oh, well, that's why they invented mops."

Garfield placed the baking dish in the oven.

"I wonder what temperature I should set the oven at?" he said.

Again Odie tried to give the cookbook to Garfield.

"That won't be necessary, Odie. I already figured it out for myself. The faster the cookies cook, the sooner I eat. So I'll just crank the temperature up as high as it will go."

Garfield turned the oven to its highest setting. Then he waited…and waited…and waited. Finally he could wait no longer.

"Two whole minutes have gone by," moaned Garfield as he flung open the oven door to look inside. "And they're still not done!"

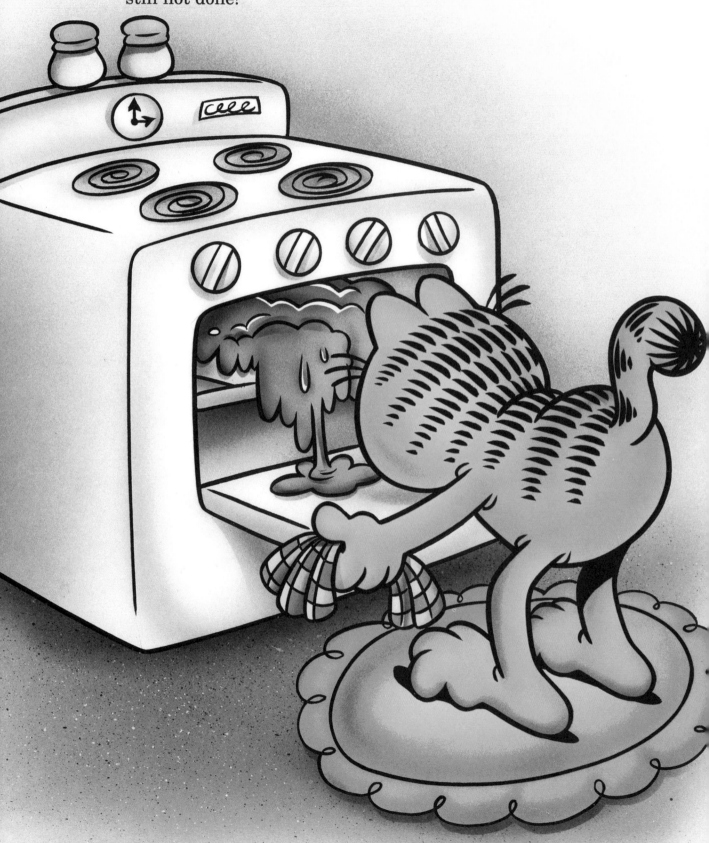

Garfield's impatience was growing—and so was his appetite.

"This is torture," he groaned. "There's got to be a faster way."

He paused for a moment to think.

"I've got it!" cried Garfield. "I'll use the microwave!"

Garfield quickly reached inside the oven and grabbed the baking dish.

"AAAYYY!!!" screamed Garfield as he dropped the dish, which was very hot. "Nice going, Odie. Why didn't you remind me to use the oven mitts? What kind of chef's helper are you, anyway?"

"Hunh?" said Odie.

"Oh, that's right," said Garfield. "You're the not-too-bright kind."

Garfield shoved the baking dish into the microwave and began pushing buttons.

"Sound the alarm, Odie! I'm on a mission. I'm microwaving these half-baked cookies. Battle stations! Give me warp speed! I want maximum power!"

The microwave whirred and hummed. "Any minute now," thought Garfield, "I'll be munching on delicious lasagna cookies!"

Suddenly there was a loud *KA-BOOM!* Off shot the microwave door and out sprang a super-gigantic Cookie Blob!

"Oh, no!" shrieked Garfield. "I've created a monster! It's Frankencookie! Run for it, Odie!"

Garfield and Odie raced out of the kitchen and hid in the hall closet. The Cookie Blob oozed after them.

Garfield peeked out of the closet. "Look, Odie. That overgrown biscuit is as slow as molasses. Which reminds me—I still haven't eaten. Anyway, what do we do now?"

"Arf," replied Odie.

"Somehow I knew you'd say that."

Meanwhile, the Cookie Blob was creeping toward them.
It was getting closer...and closer...and closer!
   "It's got us cornered!" shouted Garfield. "Quick, Odie!
Grab the vacuum cleaner! We'll bag the creature before it
gets us!"

Odie flipped on the vacuum and aimed it at the Cookie Blob.

"*SLUURRP! SLUURRP! SLUURRP!*" went the vacuum cleaner.

But it was useless. The Cookie Blob was too big and powerful. It swallowed the vacuum cleaner in one big gulp!

"What now?" asked Garfield. "You wouldn't, by any chance, have a large spatula on you?"

Odie shook his head.

"If we don't think of something soon, my little snack is going to make a snack out of us!"

Suddenly Garfield got an idea.
"That's it!" he cried. "I have the answer. I'm going to take matters into my own paws. More precisely, I'm going to take matters into my own *jaws!*"

The Cookie Blob was almost on top of them.
Garfield took a deep breath. Then he dove headfirst
into the Cookie Blob.
"CHOMP! CHEW! GOBBLE! GULP!"
The battle raged on. Odie watched in awe.

With each bite Garfield took, the Blob grew
smaller...and smaller...and smaller—and Garfield grew
larger...and larger...and larger! At last, the Cookie Blob
was no more. Garfield had done it. He had eaten the Blob
and saved the day!

There was only one problem—now Garfield was as big as a blimp!

"Don't just stand there, Odie. Do something!"

Odie did the only thing he could think of. He congratulated Garfield with a pat on the back.
"BURP!"
Garfield flew around the room like a runaway balloon.

"Excuse me," said Garfield. "It must have been something I ate."

His size was now back to normal—at least, normal for Garfield.

"Well, Odie, that's the way the Cookie Blob crumbles. But let this be a lesson to you. From now on you should always follow directions. If we had used a recipe, we could have saved ourselves a lot of trouble. And speaking of trouble…we'd better hurry and clean up this mess before Jon gets home. You mop…I'll stand lookout."

That evening, Jon came home.

"Hey, boys, I'm back!" he yelled as he walked into the
house. "I felt bad about leaving you alone all day, so I
brought you a special dinner. And to top it off, I even
brought you some cookies!"

"Oh, no, not cookies!" groaned Garfield. "I'm full. I'm
stuffed. I couldn't possibly eat another bite. Of course,
that's never stopped me before!"

1-2-3 Party Cupcakes

Garfield learned about following directions the hard way. Here are directions for turning everyday cupcakes into special occasion treats, the easy way, if you follow the steps.

You'll have fun decorating these cupcakes—and even more fun eating them! You will need a box of ready-made cupcakes that have soft, fluffy icing and the ingredients listed for each design. Then try to make up some designs of your own. You can use any kind of goody you wish: gumdrops, jelly beans, nuts, raisins, candied fruit slices, sprinkles—just use your imagination!

BUTTERFLY CUPCAKES
You'll need:

Chocolate wafer cookies
Gumdrops
Black shoestring licorice

1. Break the cookies into halves.

2. Press the curved edge of two cookie halves into the frosting on each cupcake.

3. Use small gumdrops for the eyes and black shoestring licorice for the antennae.

CLOWN CUPCAKES

You'll need:

Ice-cream cones
Hard circle candies
Coconut or chocolate sprinkles
Candy-coated chocolates
Gumdrops
Cinnamon candies

1. Push the open end of an ice-cream cone into the frosting for the clown's hat.

2. Use hard circle candies for the ears and bits of coconut or chocolate sprinkles for fringes of hair.

3. Finish with candy-coated chocolates for the eyes, a gumdrop for the nose, and cinnamon candies for the mouth.

FLOWERPOT CUPCAKES

You'll need:

Lollipops
Green leaf gumdrops

1. Trim the lollipop sticks by about one inch—they should not go all the way through the bottoms of the cupcakes.

2. Insert a lollipop in the center of each cupcake.

3. Use green leaf gumdrops for leaves.